WELCOME TO
PASSPORT TO READING
A beginning reader's ticket to a brand-new world!

Every book in this program is designed to build read-along and read-alone skills, level by level, through engaging and enriching stories. As the reader turns each page, he or she will become more confident with new vocabulary, sight words, and comprehension.

These PASSPORT TO READING levels will help you choose the perfect book for every reader.

READING TOGETHER
Read short words in simple sentence structures together to begin a reader's journey.

READING OUT LOUD
Encourage developing readers to sound out words in more complex stories with simple vocabulary.

READING INDEPENDENTLY
Newly independent readers gain confidence reading more complex sentences with higher word counts.

READY TO READ MORE
Readers prepare for chapter books with fewer illustrations and longer paragraphs.

This book features sight words from the educator-supported Dolch Sight Words List. This encourages the reader to recognize commonly used vocabulary words, increasing reading speed and fluency.

For more information, please visit passporttoreadingbooks.com.

Enjoy the journey!

Cover design by Elaine Lopez-Levine.

Little, Brown and Company
Hachette Book Group
1290 Avenue of the Americas, New York, NY 10104
Visit us at LBYR.com

First Edition: June 2018

Little, Brown and Company is a division of Hachette Book Group, Inc.
The Little, Brown name and logo are trademarks of Hachette Book Group, Inc.

The publisher is not responsible for websites (or their content) that are not owned by the publisher.

Library of Congress Control Number 2018936313

ISBNs: 978-0-316-47606-5 (pbk.), 978-0-316-48709-2 (Scholastic edition)
978-0-316-47603-4 (ebook), 978-0-316-47604-1 (ebook),
978-0-316-47605-8 (ebook)

Printed in the United States of America

CW

10 9 8 7 6 5 4 3 2 1

Passport to Reading titles are leveled by independent reviewers applying the standards developed by Irene Fountas and Gay Su Pinnell in *Matching Books to Readers*: *Using Leveled Books in Guided Reading*, Heinemann, 1999.

Meet the Cast!

Adapted by Jonathan Evans
Inspired by the film *Teen Titans Go! to the Movies*
Directed by Aaron Horvath and Peter Rida Michail
Screenplay by Michael Jelenic and Aaron Horvath
Based on characters from DC

LITTLE, BROWN AND COMPANY
New York   Boston

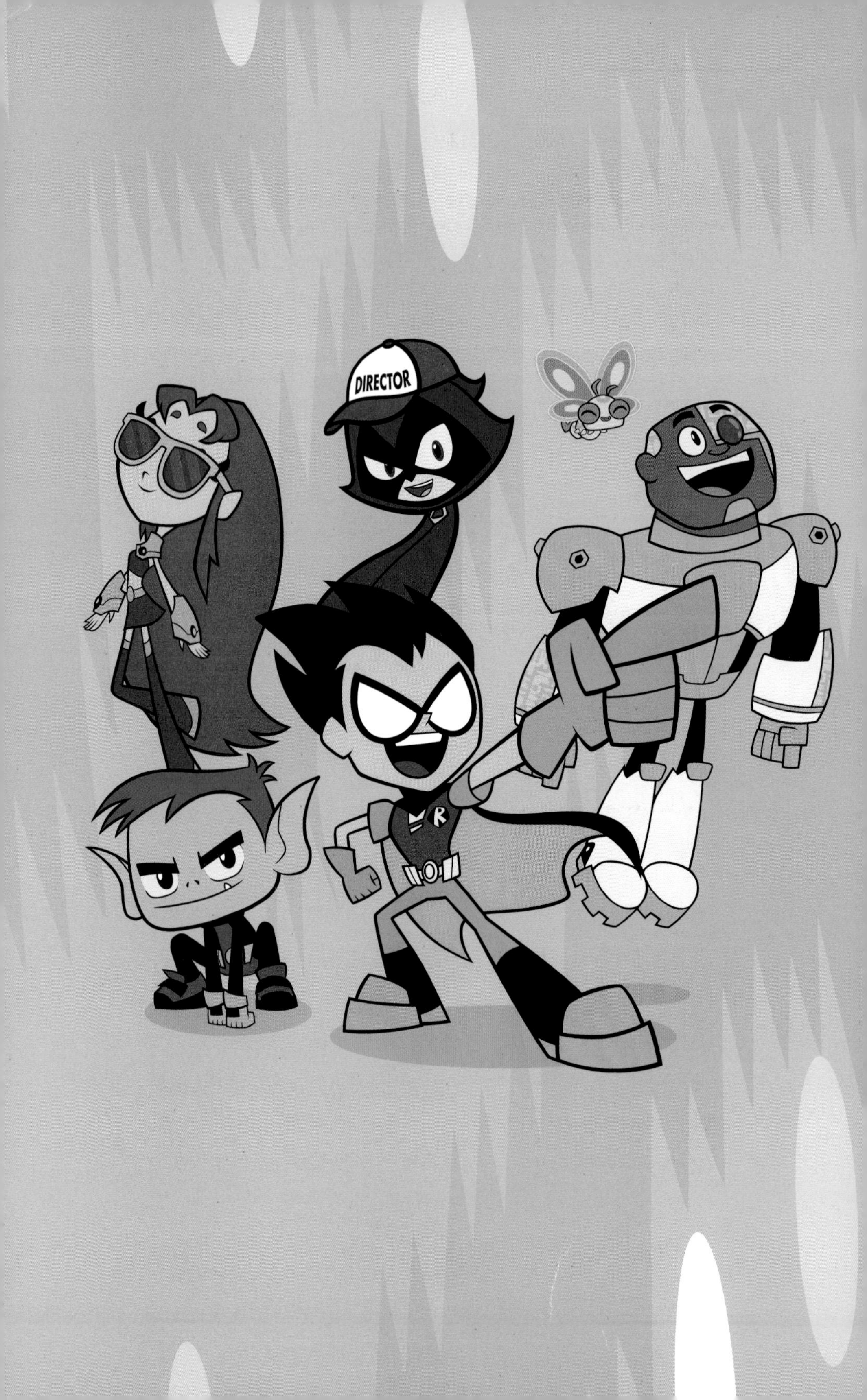
DIRECTOR

Attention, Teen Titans fans!
Look for these words when you read
this book. Can you spot them all?

attack

kitty

gorilla

director

Oh no—Jump City is under attack. Balloon Man is robbing the bank!

"Ha! Time to inflate my bank account!" he says.

The army cannot protect the city.
But maybe someone else can.

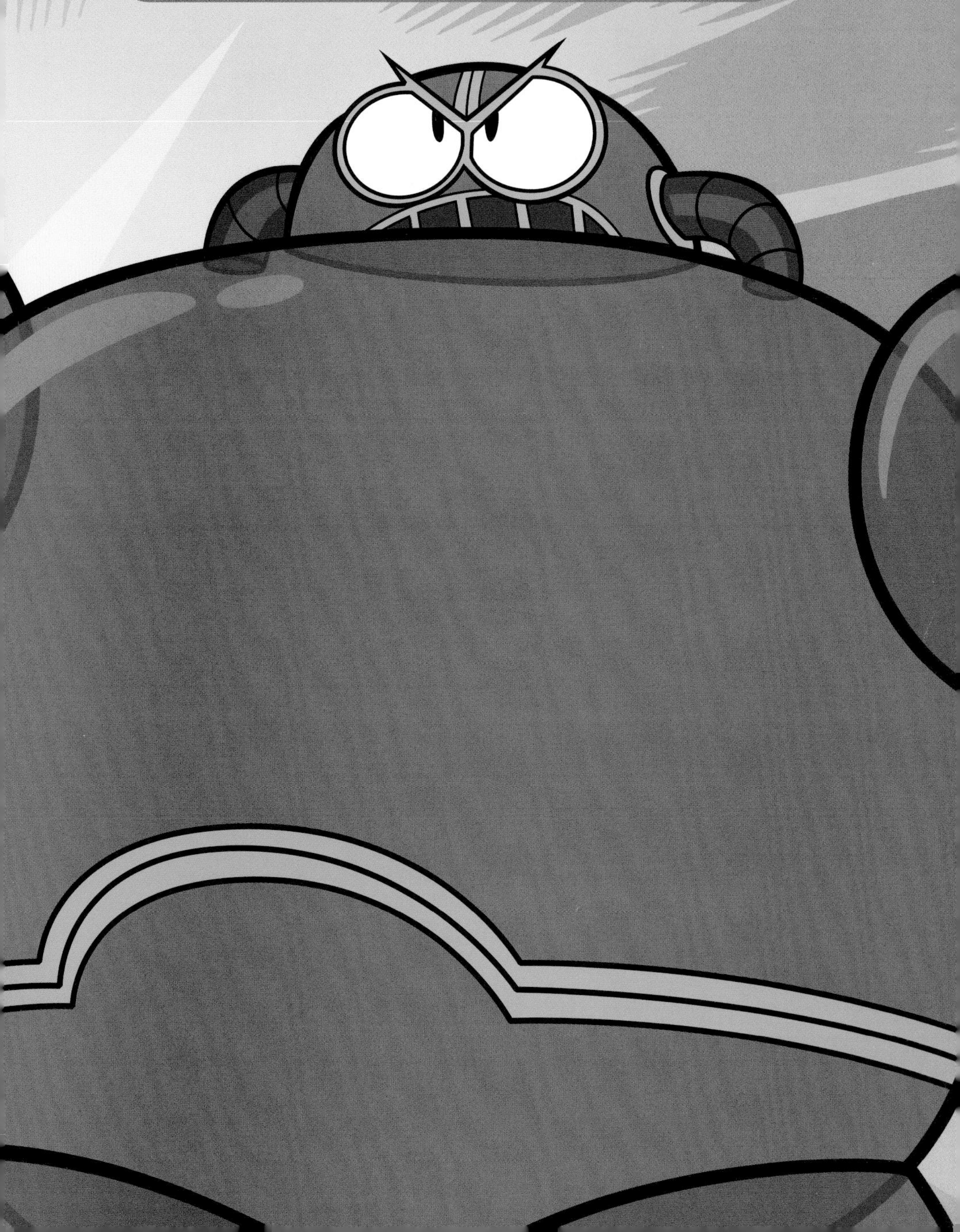

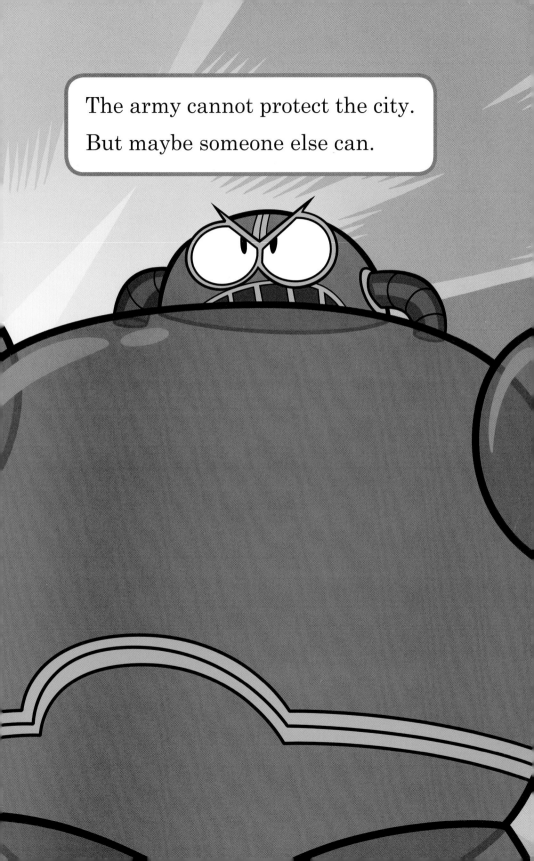

It is Robin, Starfire, Beast Boy,
Raven, and Cyborg.

They form the super hero
team called the Teen Titans!

TEEN TITANS, GO!

The Teen Titans jump
in to save the day!

"Ha-ha! Time to play!"
yells Balloon Man.

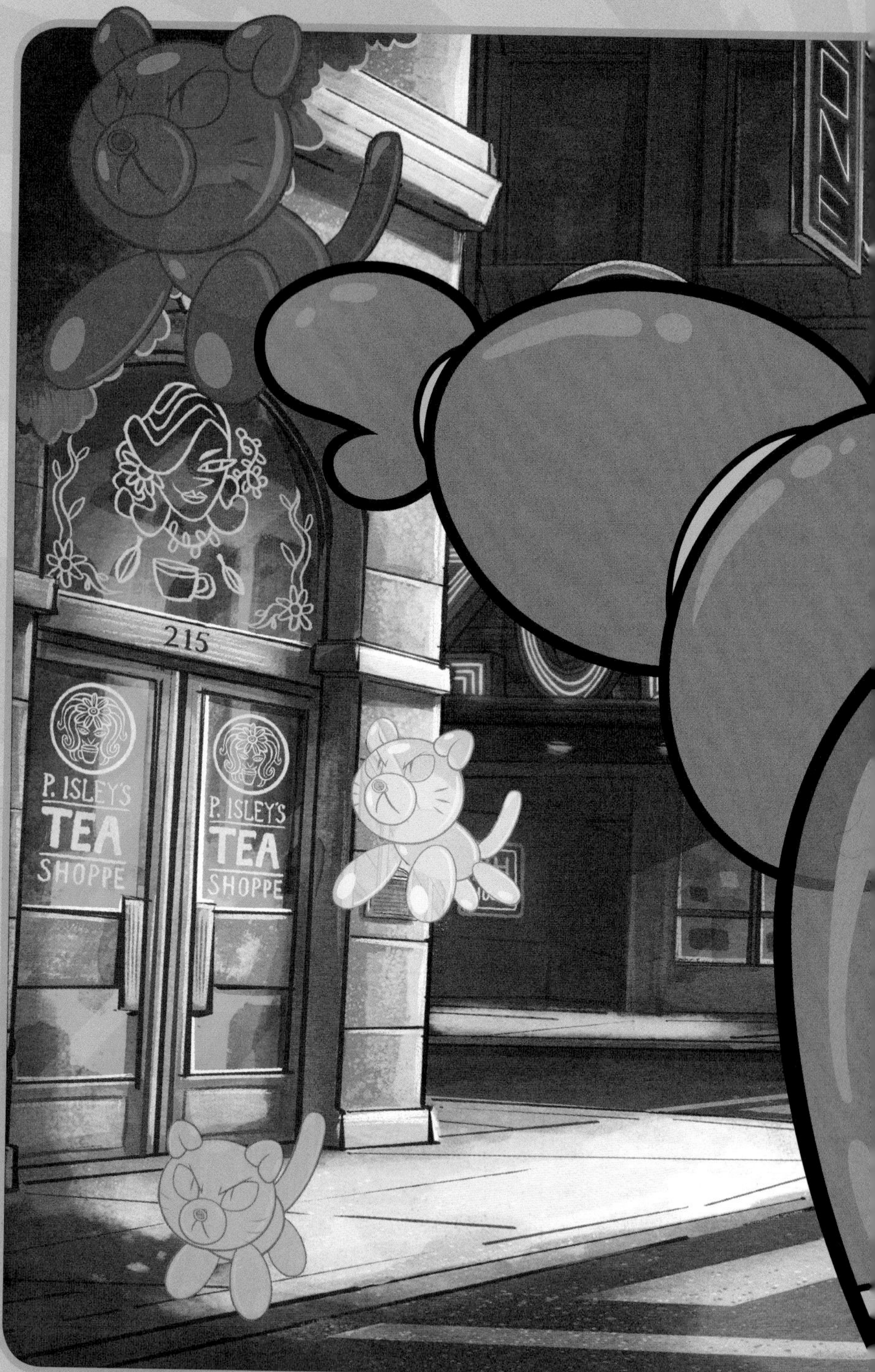
215
P. ISLEY'S
TEA
SHOPPE
P. ISLEY'S
TEA
SHOPPE

Balloon Man attacks the
team with balloon cats!
He throws the huge animals.

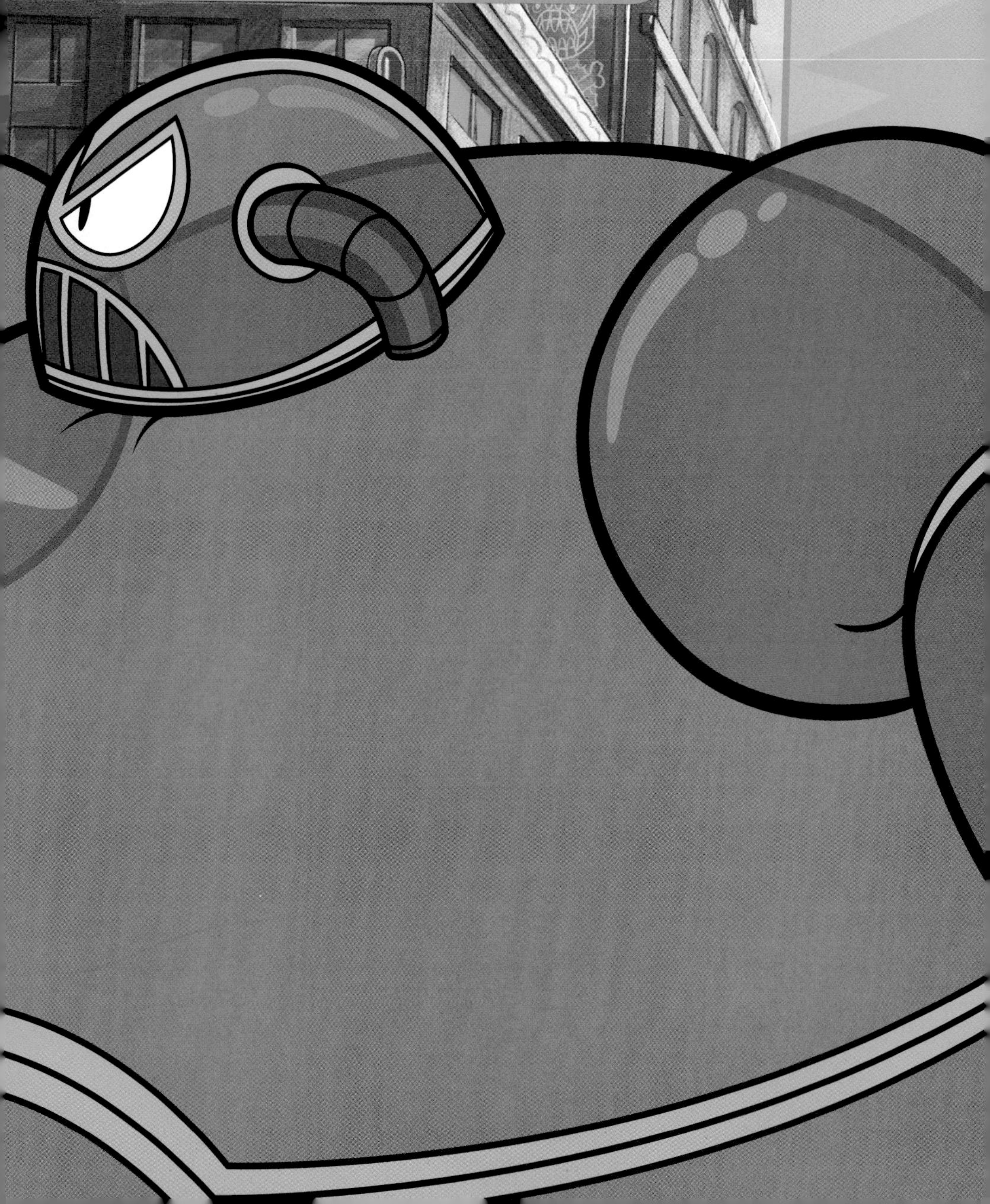

"Kitty!" yells Starfire. She loves cats of all shapes and sizes.

She thinks they are so cute! She gives one of the balloons a big hug!

"Wait a minute," says Balloon Man. "You are really young for the Justice League."

"Do we look like the Justice League to you?" Cyborg says.
"Then who are you?" Balloon Man asks the Titans.

Robin smiles.
He knows his team is ready
to stop Balloon Man.
"Titans, say hello!"

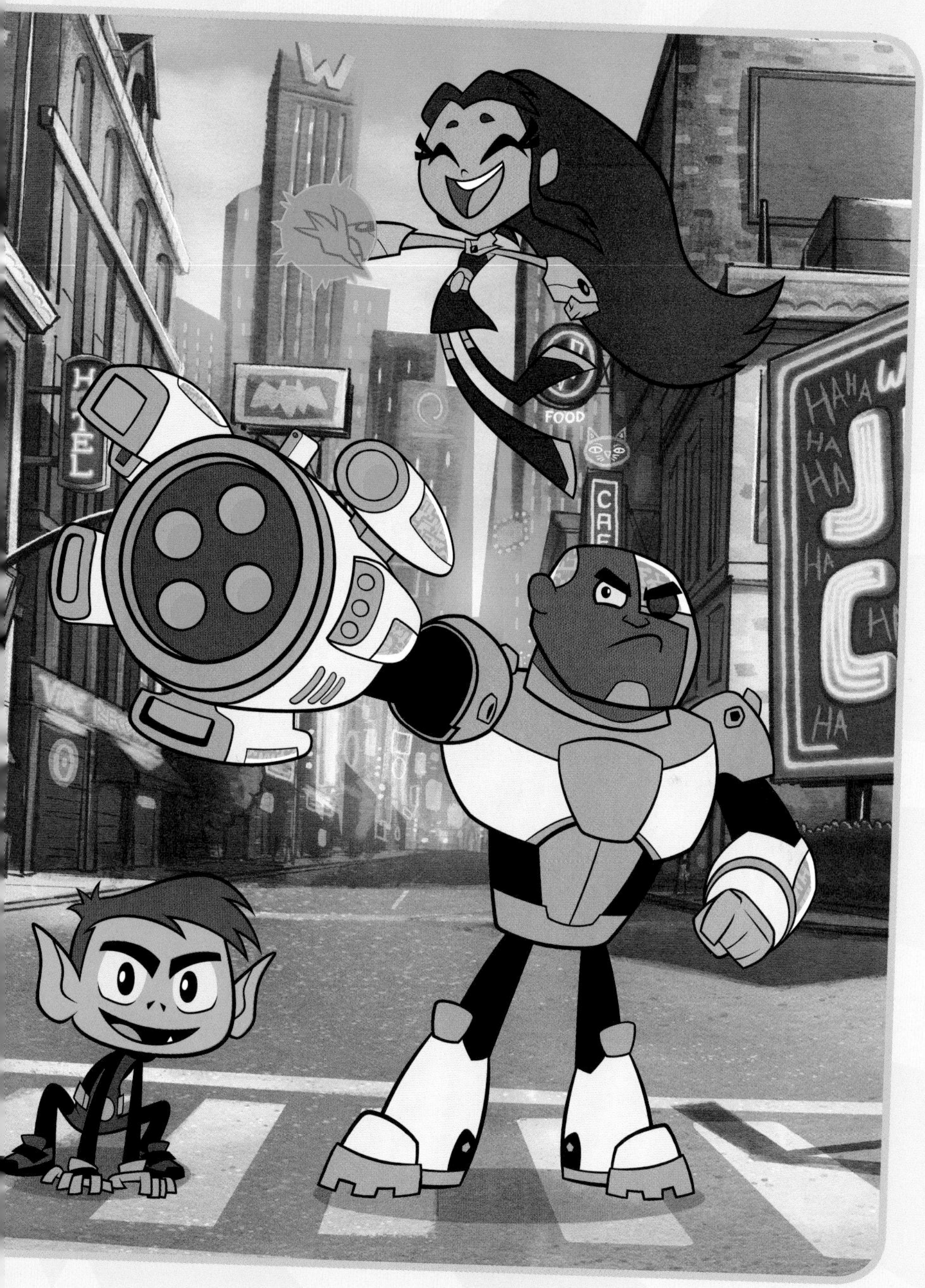
FOOD
HAHA
HA
HA
HA
HA

Beast Boy can turn
into an animal.

BEAST BOY

Sometimes he is a cat.
Sometimes he is a dog.
He loves to turn into
a gorilla!

Starfire is an alien princess. She can fly and is super-strong. She shoots energy blasts from her hands and eyes!

STARFIRE

Cyborg is half human and half robot.
He is great with machines.

Raven uses magic to cast spells. She says, "Azarath Metrion ZINTHOS!" to make her powers work.

RAVEN

ROBIN

Robin is the leader of the Teen Titans.

He is a great fighter.

He has many gadgets to help him
stop crime.

Balloon Man does not care about the Teen Titans.
He leaves with a safe while the Teen Titans are talking about themselves.

Suddenly, the Justice League appears to help stop Balloon Man.

"You are too late," says Beast Boy.
"We already took down
Balloon Man," adds Raven.

"So...do you want to hang out?"

Robin asks.

He is a big fan of the Justice League.

"Sorry, kid," Green Lantern says. "We have to watch the new Batman movie."

Green Lantern uses his power ring to make things with green light. He is too nice to tell the Titans that their villain left.

"We are all really sorry,"
says Superman.
He can fly and is very strong.
He is also very kind.

The Justice League leaves
for the theater.
The Teen Titans head to the
red-carpet event.

All the best super heroes have
movies made about them.
"We have to see that movie,"
says Robin.

Wonder Woman
is already there!

Everyone loves Wonder Woman.
She is very strong and uses
a magic lasso.

Batman is there, too!
He has fancy gadgets,
and he taught Robin how
to be a super hero.

The Teen Titans even see
Jade Wilson.
She is the director of the movie!

Robin hopes she will
make a movie about him.
Robin wants to be a star!

The Teen Titans are so excited to go to the movies!
But they are not famous enough to get inside.

So the Titans will go to Hollywood to get their own movie made!